Roof Octopus

By Lucy Branam

Illustrated by Rogério Coelho

It started with a tap at the window that woke Nora up.
Out she looked, and there it sat.

An octopus on her apartment building.

A BIG one.

She rushed from her room and went to tell her parents.

In the kitchen, her father was making waffles and her mother was pulling out the breakfast plates. Her baby sister sat in her high chair. She was pointing out the window.

Nora cleared her throat. "Excuse me, there's an octopus on our apartment."

Her father stopped pouring batter and looked out the window. "An octopus **ON** our apartment?"

Her mother looked out too. "I don't see anything." Then a tentacle dropped down from above and wrapped itself around the fire escape railing.

"See," Nora said. "There's an octopus out there."

Her family and neighbors quickly gathered outside for a better look.
Everyone started talking at once.

Nora's mother said, "I wonder if it's lost."

"It might be part of a migration," her father said.

"I think someone needs to call the Coast Guard about this," said Mr. Dodson.

Nora said nothing. She only waved at the octopus. It waved back.

"If we ignore it, maybe it will go away," suggested the landlord. So they all went on to work and school and tried not to make eye contact with it.

But the octopus stayed there all day.

And through the night, too.

The next day, Mr. Dodson was washing his car. The octopus reached out a long, strong tentacle, took a soggy sponge, and helped him. Which was a very nice thing for it to do.

"It seems like a neighborly sort of octopus,"
said the landlord with a shrug.

And the octopus was:

It pulled weeds from flower boxes.

It walked Abe McIntyre's dogs.

It helped the mailman deliver mail.

It carried Mr. and Mrs. Carmen up to their fourth-story room.

It held the door open for Nora's parents when their arms were full of groceries.

And, once or twice, it rocked her baby sister to sleep.

But what it liked to do best of all was be a swing for Nora and her friends.

"I like you," Nora told the octopus one evening when it came to wish her good night. "Would you come to school for show-and-tell sometime? This Friday?" The octopus slipped a tentacle into the room. Nora shook it. "It's a deal, then," she said. The octopus slipped its tentacle back out and shut her window for the night.

When Nora woke up, the octopus was gone.

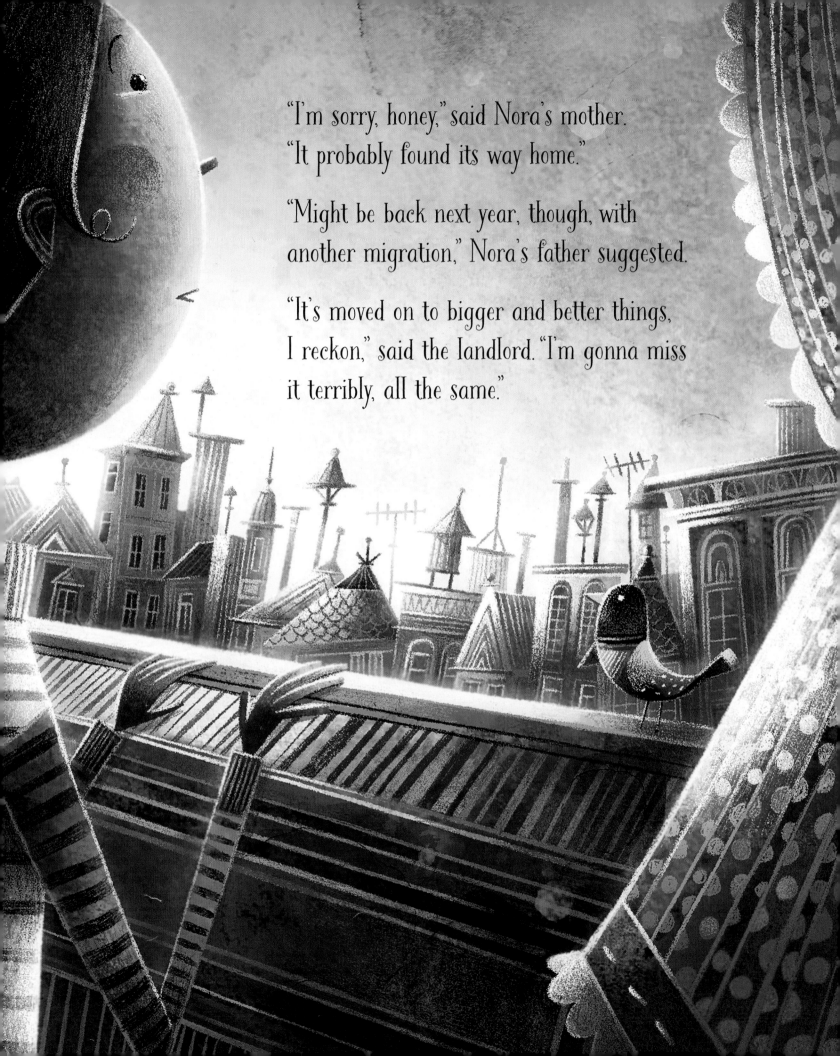

"I'm sorry, honey," said Nora's mother. "It probably found its way home."

"Might be back next year, though, with another migration," Nora's father suggested.

"It's moved on to bigger and better things, I reckon," said the landlord. "I'm gonna miss it terribly, all the same."

Nora said nothing and went on to school that day.

And the next one.

Until Friday.

While Nora was doing
her math, there was a tap
at the window.

Out she looked, and there it sat.

The octopus on her
SCHOOL.

For Poppy, who loved to tell a story.
—Lucy

An octopus has several arms, so I'll give three hugs.
Gabriel, Pedro and Laís, my dear children, this is for you.
—Rogério

Sleeping Bear Press®
2395 South Huron Parkway, Suite 200
Ann Arbor, MI 48104
www.sleepingbearpress.com

Printed and bound in the United States.

10 9 8 7 6 5 4 3 2 1

Library of Congress Cataloging-in-Publication Data

Names: Branam, Lucy, author. | Coelho, Rogério , illustrator.
Title: Roof octopus / written by Lucy Branam ; illustrated by Rogério Coelho.
Description: Ann Arbor, MI : Sleeping Bear Press, [2017] | Summary: Nora is
the first to notice a very large octopus on top of her apartment building,
which proves to be a very good neighbor but leaves all too soon.
Identifiers: LCCN 2017006065 | ISBN 9781585369973
Subjects: | CYAC: Octopuses—Fiction. | Neighborliness—Fiction. |
Apartment houses—Fiction.
Classification: LCC PZ7.1.B7514 Roo 2017 | DDC [E]—dc23
LC record available at https://lccn.loc.gov/2017006065

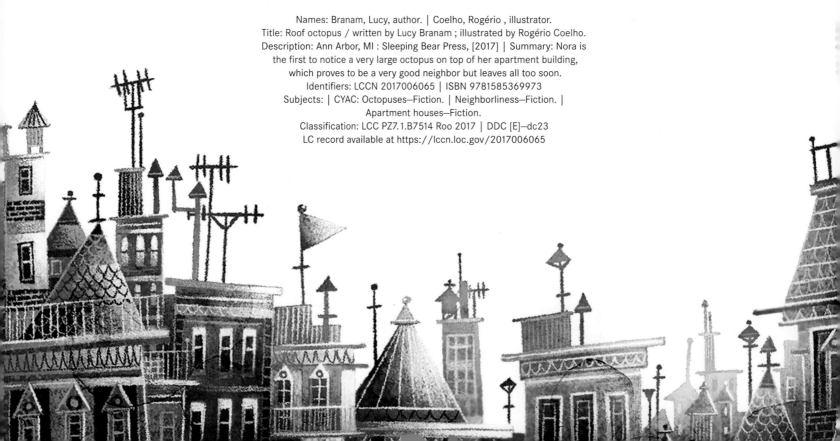